A TEMPLAR BOOK

First published in the UK in 2011 by Templar Publishing,
an imprint of The Templar Company Limited,
The Granary, North Street, Dorking, Surrey, RH4 1DN, UK
www.templarco.co.uk

ISBN 978-1-84877-218-2

Printed in Malaysia

templar publishing
www.templarco.co.uk

OWEN ★ DAVEY

KNIGHT NIGHT

For a knight, going to bed...

I go down the hallway...

and climb the stairs.

Then I have a bath...

and brush my teeth.

I say goodnight to Rex...

BYE

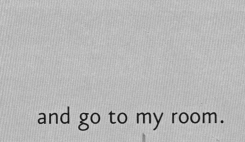

and go to my room.

I tidy away my things...

and turn out the lights.

Such a great adventure makes me very tired.

Even a knight needs a good night's sleep.